Harry *and the* Dinosaurs *say* 'Raahh!'

Written by Ian Whybrow

Illustrated by Adrian Reynolds

Mum had her coat on,
but Harry was being slow.
They were going to see
Mr Drake, the dentist.

Harry was only a bit scared.
That was because of Sam
showing him her filling.

Harry wanted to take his dinosaurs,
but they were hiding all over the place.
He called all their names.

He said, "Get in the bucket, my Stegosaurus."
And out came Stegosaurus from under
the pillow.

He said, "Get in the bucket, my Triceratops."
And out came Triceratops from inside
the drawer.

And one by one, Apatosaurus and Scelidosaurus and Anchisaurus all came out of their hiding places and they jumped into the bucket.

All except for Tyrannosaurus. He didn't want
to go because he had a lot of teeth.
He thought Mr Drake might do drilling on them.

Harry said, "Don't worry, because when we get there,
I shall press a magic button on my bucket,
and that will make you grow big."

In the waiting room, the nurse said,
"Hello, Harry. Are you a good boy?"
Harry said, "I am, but my dinosaurs bite."

Then Mr Drake called,
"Next please!"

The nurse took Harry into Mr Drake's room.
Harry wasn't sure about the big chair. He thought
maybe that was where Mr Drake did the drilling.

"Come and have a ride in my chair," said Mr Drake.
"It goes up and down."

Harry didn't want to ride.

"Would one of your dinosaurs like a go?"
asked Mr Drake.

Harry put Tyrannosaurus on the chair.
He whispered to him not to worry,
then he pressed the magic button . . .
Tyrannosaurus grew VERY BIG!

"Open wide," said Mr Drake,
and then he turned around . . .

"RAAAAHH!" said Tyrannosaurus.
"Help!" cried Mr Drake, hiding behind the door. "Harry, what shall I do?"

Harry pressed the magic button.
Straight away, Tyrannosaurus
went back to being bucket-sized.

Harry felt safer now about getting
into the chair, so he climbed in with
his bucket. Then Harry and his dinosaurs
all had a ride together.
They opened their mouths wide for
Mr Drake and all went, 'RAAAAHH!'
Mr Drake said, "What a lot of teeth!
Will they bite me?"
Harry said, "They only bite drills."

"You are all good brushers," said Mr Drake,
"so no drills today, only a look
and a rinse."

All the dinosaurs liked riding and they liked rinsing.
   "Another bucket of mouthwash, Joan!"
called Mr Drake.

Going home, Mum let Harry choose a book
from the library for being so good.

"Let's have a shark book!" said Harry.

"RAAAAHH!" said the dinosaurs.
"Sharp teeth! We like sharks!"

ENDOSAURUS